Pony Poems for Little Pony Lovers

Poems by Cari Meister

Ponies by Sara Rhys

Beach Lane Books · New York London Toronto Sydney New Delhi

Sugar Plum

My pony knows me.
He hears me when I come.
He lifts his head.
He neighs my name.

He is my Sugar Plum.

Kicking Kate

I have a piebald pony.

She is really great.

I have a piebald pony.

Her name is Kicking Kate.

She doesn't kick in the pasture.

She doesn't kick in her stall.

She doesn't kick at the doggies.

In fact, she doesn't kick at all!

Bay Horse

Bay horse, bay horse,
carry me to town.
You will get a carrot.
I will get a crown.

I Want to Be a Cowboy

I want to be a cowboy.
Yes, sir, I do.
I want to be a cowboy.
Yes, sir, it's true.

I want to be a cowboy.
Yes, sir, I do.
I want to be a cowboy.
Yes, sir, like you!

My Friend George

My friend George likes
green grass,
red apples,
blue buckets full of food,
and a friend who will run and play
day after day.

Gentle Gwen

Gentle Gwen is a giant.
She's taller than a tree.
But I'm not scared of her.
And she's not scared of me.

Nibbles

I am a treat machine—
at least that's what he thinks.
He nibbles at my hair.
He nibbles at my sleeves.
He nibbles and nibbles and nibbles and nibbles—
until a treat's released!

Sweet Little Penny

Sweet little Penny
looks so cute and nice.
But sweet little Penny . . .

bucked me off—
twice!

Sir William

In my dreams,
I am a knight.
Sir William is my steed.
When a dragon roars to life,
we always take the lead.

Princess

I am a pretty little pony,
as pretty as can be.
All the girls at riding school
are crazy over me!

Sheena

Sheena likes to race.
She'll race anything that runs.
A cat, a dog, a donkey—anything will do.
I don't care what she races,
'cause I like racing too!

Mare of Mine

Little white mare,
come away with me.
We will run and dance and sing
a happy harmony.

A-Riding We Will Go

A-riding we will go,
a-riding we will go.
Up and down the mountainside,
a-riding we will go.

Mickery, Mackery Mare

Mickery, mackery mare,
the horse flies up in the air.
The boy in brown
then brings her down.
Mickery, mackery mare.

Molasses and Oats
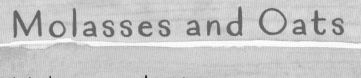

Molasses and oats—
oh, so sweet.
Come, little pony.
Come and eat.

Sleepy Mare

Yellow,

orange,

blanket red.

Time to put my mare to bed.

She is sleepy.

I am too.

Starry nighttime.

Shiny.

Blue.

SHEENA

SPIRIT

LULA

PENNY

SIR WILLIAM

OLIVER

GEORGE

JACK